W9-CKE-073

Heading to the Wedding

You're invited to join Patrick and Evie on the great adventure of becoming (almost) perfect guests

Story by Sara F. Shacter

Illustrations by Christine Thornton

A Red Pebble Book
from Red Rock Press

*To Joe—my Everything—and to my parents,
who have always believed in me.—S.F.S.*

*To Scott for encouraging me to head for my dream career,
and to Jake and Hannah, my very own party professionals.—C.T.*

This book, including its illustrations, may not be reprinted, in whole or part, without consent from Red Rock Press.

Story copyright © 2006 Sara F. Shacter
Illustrations copyright © 2006 Christine Thornton
Book Design by Heather Zschock

Printed in Singapore

ISBN: 1933176-059

Red Rock Press
459 Columbus Avenue, Suite 114
New York NY 10024
www.RedRockPress.com

Library of Congress Cataloging-in-Publication Data
Shacter, Sara. Heading to the wedding / by Sara Shacter ; illustrated by Christine Thornton.
p. cm.
"A Red Pebble Book."
Summary: A family copes with getting their children ready to be good guests at a wedding.
ISBN 1-933176-05-9
[1. Behavior—Fiction. 2. Weddings—Fiction.] I. Thornton, Christine, ill. II.
Title.
PZ7.S5258Hea 2006
[E]—dc22
2005025196

Heading to the Wedding

I'm Patrick, the Party Professional.

I can shove more cake into my mouth than anyone.

I always know when to start the screaming contest.

I give excellent presents.

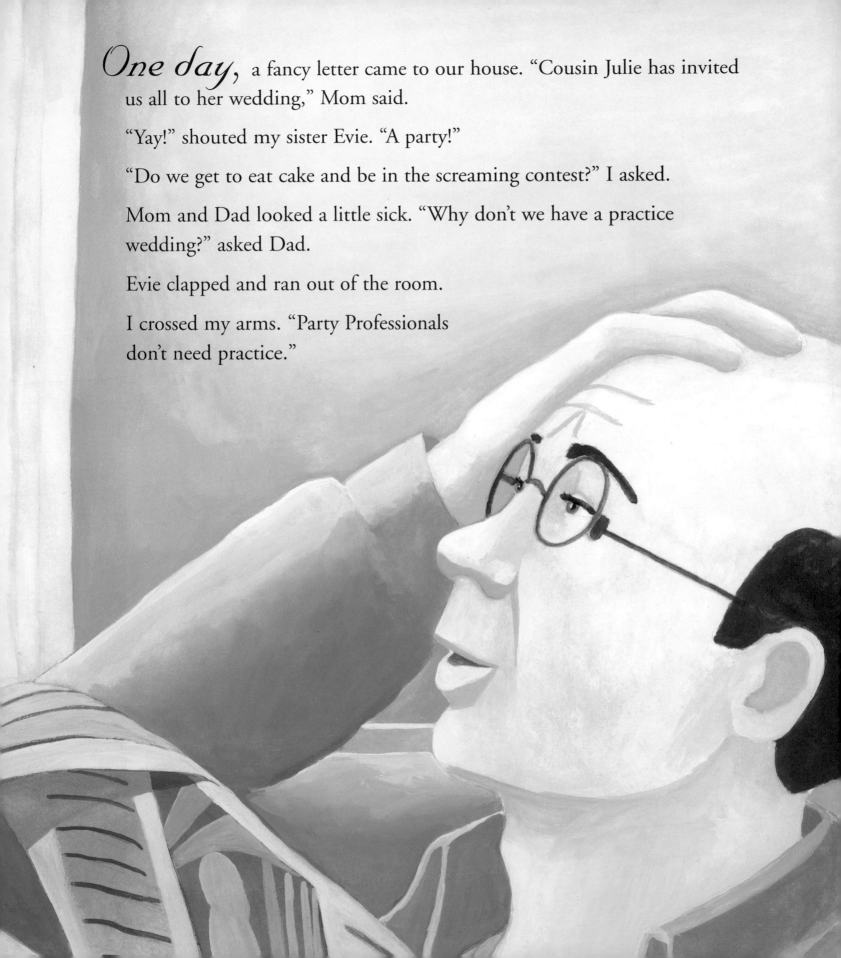

One day, a fancy letter came to our house. "Cousin Julie has invited us all to her wedding," Mom said.

"Yay!" shouted my sister Evie. "A party!"

"Do we get to eat cake and be in the screaming contest?" I asked.

Mom and Dad looked a little sick. "Why don't we have a practice wedding?" asked Dad.

Evie clapped and ran out of the room.

I crossed my arms. "Party Professionals don't need practice."

"Tell you what," said Mom, "why don't you get a few stuffed animals and action guys?"

I ran to my room and came back with a whole bunch. Then I threw them into the air and picked the ones that fell on my head: T-Rex and Dracula.

"Throwing is not part of a wedding," said Mom.

"ROAR!" I yelled. "T-rex wants to be in charge," I explained.

"Okay, T-Rex can be in charge," said Mom. "Then Dracula will be the groom, and . . . "

"I'm the bride!" shouted Evie, twirling in. She was wrapped in toilet paper.

"Right," said Mom. "Everyone else will watch."

T-rex flashed his pointy teeth
and tried to eat Evie.

"Stop!" shouted Mom. "Nobody runs at a wedding. And nobody eats anybody else."

Weddings sure sounded boring.

"The bride and groom stand in front of T-rex," said Mom. "They promise to love each other forever, and then they kiss."

"Yuck!" I said, and Evie made a face.

Mom didn't look happy.

I grabbed Dracula, stuck out my teeth, and made him say, "I promith."

Dad laughed. Mom waved her finger at him.
"The ceremony is a quiet time," she warned.

Dad said he was sorry.

"I promise too," giggled Evie. She kissed Dracula's head.
Then she started to spin like crazy.
She looked like a toilet paper tornado.

Dad covered his mouth and left before he got in trouble again.

"Now do we get to eat cake?" I asked.

Dad came out of the kitchen with a tray of tiny peanut butter sandwiches.

"Sir, Madam," he said. He sounded like his nose was stuffed up. "Would you like an hors d'oeuvre?"

"Those are sandwiches," I pointed out.

"An hors d'oeuvre," Dad explained, "is a snack before dinner."

"Wow!" I cheered. I stuffed the three biggest into my mouth.

"No fair!" whined Evie, who threw two sandwiches at my head.

"Just take the one closest to you," said Dad. "And eat it slowly."

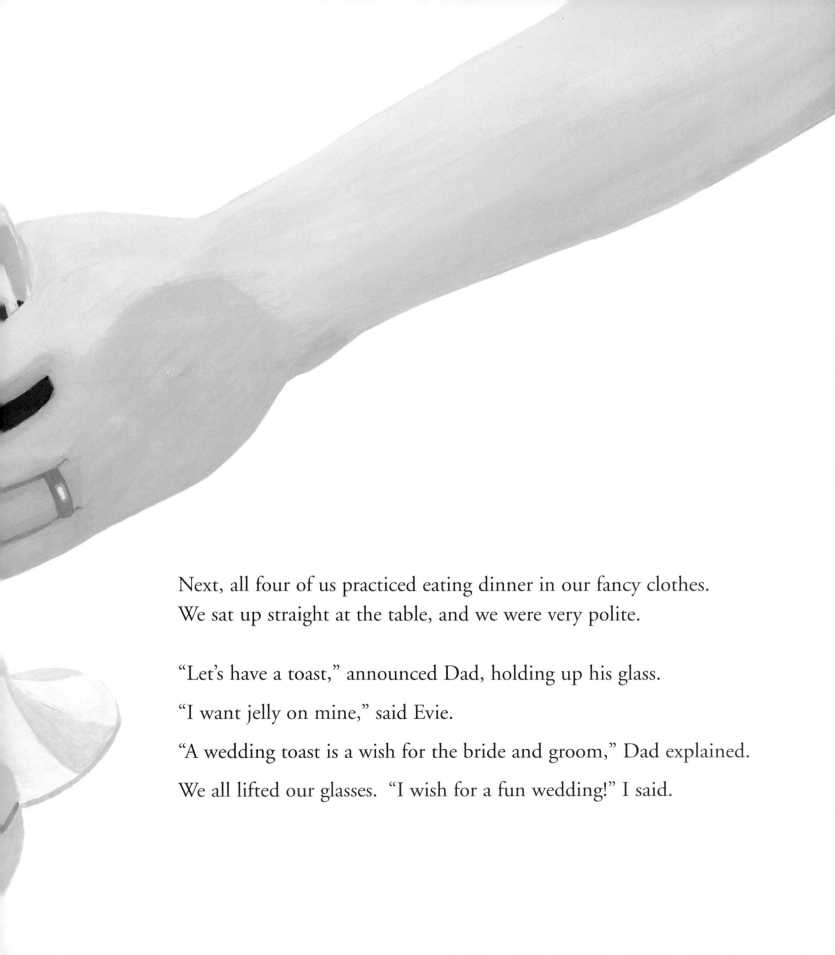

Next, all four of us practiced eating dinner in our fancy clothes.
We sat up straight at the table, and we were very polite.

"Let's have a toast," announced Dad, holding up his glass.

"I want jelly on mine," said Evie.

"A wedding toast is a wish for the bride and groom," Dad explained.

We all lifted our glasses. "I wish for a fun wedding!" I said.

Then we practiced dancing.

On the big day, it took us a while
to get ready. After all, you can't
rush Wedding Professionals.

During the ceremony,
we were very quiet.
Dad didn't giggle once.

When the hors d'oeuvres lady came by,
we took the closest ones.

At dinner we raised our glasses high for
the toast and nobody threw food.

I danced with Mom, Grandma,
Dad, Julie and even Evie.

Before dessert, Julie and her new husband,
Sam, cut the biggest cake I ever saw—
and squished it on each other's faces!

Then when Julie and Sam were ready to leave,
everyone cheered as loudly as they could and
threw birdseed at them for good luck.

Boy, cake smushing? Yelling? Throwing?
And Mom and Dad were worried about *us*?

Patrick's Dictionary of Wedding Words

BRIDE The lady who's getting married.

GROOM The guy she's marrying.

BEST MAN The groom's best friend. The best man stands next to the groom during the ceremony. Sometimes he holds the wedding rings so the groom doesn't lose them. At the reception, the best man makes a toast and tells silly stories about the groom.

BRIDAL BOUQUET The flowers the bride holds. Sometimes the bride throws it at her girl friends before she leaves. People say the girl who catches it will be the next bride. Some girls push to get the bouquet; some run away.

BRIDESMAIDS The bride's special friends. The bridesmaids dress the same. They look like toy soldiers, only fluffier.

CEREMONY The first part of the wedding, with fancy words and love promises. You have to sit still and be quiet and pretend to listen.

FLOWER GIRL A girl who walks in front of the bride and throws flower petals on the floor. Brides like walking on flowers.

GROOMSMEN The groom's pals, sometimes called Ushers. They're like bridesmaids, only they don't wear dresses.

HONEYMOON A vacation the bride and groom take after the wedding to rest up from being good.

MAID OF HONOR The bride's best friend or lady relative. (If she is married, she's called the Matron of Honor.) She stands next to the bride during the ceremony, and holds the bouquet when the groom tries to get the ring on the bride's finger.

RECEPTION The fun part with food and dancing and cake!!!

RECEPTION LINE When everyone stands in a line and tells the bride and groom that they didn't mess up. You say they looked great.

RING BEARER A boy who holds the wedding rings so the Best Man doesn't have to worry.

USHER A groomsman or someone else who tells people where to sit during the ceremony. Sometimes the bride's family sits on one side, and the groom's family sits on the other. I guess it's so they won't fight about who is better.